··· Contents ···

1. A Bit of a Surprise

It was Saturday morning and every Saturday morning Mr Primly-Proper washed his car.

Every Saturday morning Mrs Primly-Proper clipped the hedge. Their son, Jack, mowed the lawn and their daughter, Daisy, polished the gnome that stood by the garden pond.

"I've got a brilliant idea," said Mr Primly-Proper as he picked up the garden hose.

"What's that, dear?" asked Mrs Primly-Proper.

"Let's go on holiday with Aunt Doris and Uncle Douglas," said Mr Primly-Proper. "Now that they've come back from Scotland, we should all get to know each other again."

"That's a good idea," beamed Mrs Primly-Proper. "Jack and Daisy haven't seen them for years and they're bound to like the same things we do."

Jack and Daisy rolled their eyes. If Uncle Douglas and Aunt Doris liked the same things as their parents, you could bet your Rollerblades, the holiday would be twice as boring as it usually was.

At that moment a car pulled up and Uncle Douglas and Aunt Doris jumped out.

Jack and Daisy couldn't believe their eyes. Uncle Douglas was wearing a bright purple shirt.

On it was a gold tiepin in the shape
of a guitar. His hair was greased
back and as shiny as his black
pointy shoes.

Aunt Doris was wearing a tight
polka-dot top over a wide swirly
rainbow-coloured skirt. Her hair was
piled on top of her head and held up

with bunny-rabbit clips.

Mr and Mrs Primly-Proper
couldn't believe their eyes either.
Not only did Uncle Douglas and
Aunt Doris look really peculiar,
they hadn't even telephoned to say
they were coming!

"Hope you don't mind a little

surprise," called Aunt Doris. "We were on our way home from dancing classes and –"

"And I had a brilliant idea!" cried Uncle Douglas. He grabbed Aunt Doris's hand and twirled her like a top all the way up the paving-stone path to the front door.

Jack and Daisy looked at each other and grinned. Maybe Uncle Douglas and Aunt Doris were not like their own parents after all!

2. A Brilliant Idea!

"So what do you think?" said Uncle Douglas as everyone sat around the kitchen table drinking tea. "Would you come camping with us in Scotland?"

Mrs Primly-Proper looked as if her face had melted. "It's not quite what we had in mind," she said at last.

"We'd have to sleep in a tent," said Mr Primly-Proper. As he spoke, his hands made nervous fluttering movements.

"In fact, it doesn't sound like a holiday at all!" wailed Mrs Primly-Proper.

"It's not!" said Uncle Douglas. "It's an *adventure*!"

Aunt Doris smiled a curious smile. "And you will meet all sorts of interesting people."

Mr and Mrs Primly-Proper exchanged looks. They didn't want to meet all sorts of interesting people. They wanted a beach, a golf course and a nice quiet hotel.

Then Mr Primly-Proper had another brilliant idea.

The whole point of going on holiday with Uncle Douglas and Aunt Doris had been so Jack and Daisy could get to know them.

It was not so Mr and Mrs Primly-
Proper would get cold and wet,
camping.

Mr Primly-Proper patted his wife
reassuringly on her arm. What he
was about to say really was rather
extraordinary and he didn't want to
alarm her.

"Perhaps Jack and Daisy would like to go."

Jack and Daisy's eyes spun like circus plates.

They couldn't believe their luck.

"Yes, please!" they shouted at the top of their voices.

Mrs Primly-Proper squeezed her hands together and thought hard. It *was* all a little bit unexpected, but Uncle Douglas and Aunt Doris *were* family after all. Even if they did do strange things like dress up and go to dancing classes.

"Well," she began with a little smile.

"That's settled then!" cried Aunt Doris. "Jack and Daisy will come camping with us."

"When?" asked Mrs Primly-Proper, nervously.

"Now," replied Aunt Doris, firmly.

"Please!" shouted Jack and Daisy again.

They knew there was no time to lose. They had to leave before their parents changed their minds.

Mrs Primly-Proper took a deep breath to steady herself. "As long as you take woolly vests and sensible shoes," she said at last.

3. The Tea Leaves Were Right

Ten minutes later, Jack and
Daisy were sitting in the back
of their aunt and uncle's car with
their cases packed and their seat
belts fastened.

"Now, remember your manners,"

said Mr Primly-Proper, through the window.

"And send us a postcard," said Mrs Primly-Proper. She bit her lip as if she had just remembered something important. "And don't forget –"

But somehow Aunt Doris pushed

the wrong button and all the electric windows shot up.

And somehow Uncle Douglas's shiny pointed shoes slipped on to the accelerator pedal and the car roared off like a rocket.

Jack and Daisy just had time to wave!

"Phew!" said Aunt Doris, offering round a bag of gobstoppers. "It worked!"

"What worked?" asked Daisy stuffing two gobstoppers in her mouth. Jack stuffed in three!

Aunt Doris turned round. "Can you keep a secret?"

Jack and Daisy nodded. They couldn't speak because of the gobstoppers.

"Excellent!" cried Aunt Doris.
"We're not going camping, we're
going on a rescue mission."

Daisy's mouth dropped open.
"Wha –"

"And we need you to help us,"
said Uncle Douglas.

"Why uth?" gurgled Jack.

"Because Hector McHandy read

it in his tea leaves," explained Aunt
Doris.

At that moment, Uncle Douglas
stopped the car and jumped out.
"Home sweet home!" he cried.

Jack and Daisy stared at a huge
bullet-shaped silver camper truck.
Two yellow eyes glowed on its
bonnet. The sides were painted with
green fins. It looked like a sea
monster on wheels.

"We thought you lived in a
bungalow," croaked Jack.

Aunt Doris laughed. "That's
what we tell the family," she said.

Jack and Daisy walked into the
camper truck.

It was like walking into a cave!
The walls were painted grey and

looked as if they were made of rock. A table at one end was a boulder covered with a table cloth of moss. Around it, four chairs were made from flat stones.

"Make yourselves at home," said Uncle Douglas. And they disappeared through a door that was painted to look like a tunnel.

"Daisy," whispered Jack. "They're completely crazy!"

"Absolutely nuts," agreed Daisy happily.

A moment later, Uncle Douglas and Aunt Doris came back. They were dressed in shiny-blue jumpsuits with mining helmets on their heads. Tartan cloaks hung from their shoulders. And around their necks

something that looked like a
dinosaur's tooth dangled from a
leather cord.

"Wow!" cried Daisy, clapping her
hands. "I love the tooth necklace."

Uncle Douglas winked at Aunt
Doris. "The tea leaves were right,"
he cried. "Hector McHandy knew

Jack and Daisy would be the best ones for the job!"

"What job?" asked Jack.

Uncle Douglas looked serious. "A very important job," he said.

"Who is Hector Mc–" began Daisy.

But Aunt Doris was already behind the wheel. She turned the key and a great throaty engine roared into life. "Scotland here we come!" she cried.

4. Welcome to the Clan!

T he next evening, Jack and Daisy
    stood with Uncle Douglas and
Aunt Doris in front of a huge castle
halfway up a mountain.

Below them the inky black waters
of Loch Ness glittered in the setting
sun.

Uncle Douglas banged on the door. It opened with a squeal of rusty hinges.

Even though it is rude to stare, Jack and Daisy stared until their eyes crossed. In front of them stood an enormously tall man with black grizzly hair and a thick beard.

A dinosaur-sized tooth swung from a leather cord around his neck. A tartan cloak just like Uncle Douglas's and Aunt Doris's hung from his shoulders.

"You have arrived just in time!" he thundered. "Welcome, Jack and Daisy! I am Hector McHandy, Head of the McHandy clan. Follow me!"

They walked into a great panelled room with a high wooden gallery. A huge chandelier dangled from the ceiling.

In front of a blazing fire stood the rest of the McHandy clan. They all wore identical tartan cloaks and dinosaur-tooth necklaces.

Without a word, Hector

McHandy took Jack and Daisy by the hand and led them up the stairs to the gallery.

Daisy couldn't keep quiet another moment. "Excuse me," she began.

Then she stopped because Hector McHandy had hooked the great chandelier and was pulling it towards them as if it were a tyre swing on the end of a rope!

Jack felt his mouth drop open. "I don't believe this," he muttered.

A moment later, Jack and Daisy were perched on the chandelier, holding on as tight as they could.

"Ready?" whispered Hector McHandy.

"Ready," choked Jack and Daisy.

"Ladies and Gentlemen!" roared
Hector McHandy.

Below them the room went silent.
You could have heard a kilt rustle.

"As you know, it is the McHandy custom to welcome special guests in a special way!"

Then he gave the chandelier a great shove and Jack and Daisy sailed backwards and forwards across the room.

It was better than the best ride at a funfair!

"Yippee!" shouted Daisy.

"Wow!" yelled Jack.

"Welcome!" cried Hector. And everyone clapped.

Then Hector McHandy caught the chandelier and led Jack and Daisy downstairs.

5. Who Are the SAD Mob?

Hector McHandy sat down, untied the giant tooth from the cord around his neck and banged it on the top of the long table.

At last! thought Jack and Daisy. *Now* we'll find out what's going on!

"Our plans to rescue Loopy have changed," announced Hector McHandy.

A ripple of astonishment went round the table.

"Who's Loopy?" whispered Jack to Daisy.

"Is something wrong with Loopy?" cried Aunt Doris.

"There's nothing wrong with Loopy," replied Hector McHandy. "It's the SAD mob. Someone must have tipped them off."

Daisy saw her chance. "Who are the SAD mob?" she asked quickly.

"SAD means Stuff And Display," explained Aunt Doris through clenched teeth. "This mob searches the country for strange creatures.

And when they find them –" She stopped as if she couldn't carry on.

"They stuff and display them on their clubhouse wall," said Uncle Douglas in a low growl.

Jack was about to ask exactly what kind of strange creatures they were talking about, when Hector McHandy banged the dinosaur tooth on the table.

"There's no time to lose!" he cried. "The SAD mob are down by the loch. Loopy must be rescued tonight!"

There was a split-second silence.

"Is the great haggis cooked?" asked Uncle Douglas.

"Is the giant bottle ready?" asked Aunt Doris.

Hector McHandy nodded. "We must prepare Jack and Daisy."

Jack went white and looked at Daisy.

Daisy turned green and looked at Jack.

The chandelier ride was great. Now it was beginning to sound as if

they were going to be eaten for
pudding!

Hector stood up.

"Summon the wrinkled retainer!"
he cried.

"What's a wrinkled retainer?"
whispered Jack to Daisy.

"Every castle has one," explained Uncle Douglas.

At that moment, an old man hobbled up to Jack and Daisy, grinned a toothless grin and held out two large cardboard boxes.

Jack and Daisy's hands shook as they opened them.

But they needn't have worried.

Inside was a tartan cloak and a huge tooth on a leather cord. As Jack and Daisy put them on, everyone around the table stood up and cheered.

Hector McHandy grinned a tombstone teeth grin and patted Jack and Daisy on the shoulder. "You are now honorary members of the McHandy clan!"

6. Who Is Loopy?

Late that night, Jack and Daisy
followed Uncle Douglas and
Aunt Doris up a narrow path.
Below them the waters of Loch
Ness shone silver in the moonlight.

"Where are we going and who's
Loopy?" asked Jack.

Aunt Doris adjusted her helmet light. "We're going to a secret cave," she said in a low voice. "And –"

"Doris!" croaked Uncle Douglas. "Look! It's the SAD mob."

Jack and Daisy and Aunt Doris turned. A line of lanterns flickered along the side the loch.

"We must rescue Loopy," said Aunt Doris in a choked voice. "Before it's too late!"

"Who is Loopy?" asked Daisy.

"Loopy's our baby," crooned Aunt Doris. "He's a –"

Suddenly Uncle Douglas ducked into a cave and began to sing.

"*Old MacDonald had a farm,*
E-I-E-I-O!

And on that farm he had a little
   monster.
E-I-E-I-O!"

From the back of the cave came
a low watery chortle. It sounded like
a giant blowing bubbles in his bath.

The hairs on the back of Daisy's
neck stood on end.

Jack's knees were knocking under
his cloak.

"Aunt Doris," said Daisy, slowly. "Are we here to help you rescue a baby *monster*?"

"He's so adorable," cooed Aunt Doris. "Such *sweet* yellow eyes."

She unpacked a giant baby bottle of weak tea. "You see, we found him just after he'd hatched out of his egg. Uncle Douglas called him Loopy because he looped his little

green tail around his finger and wouldn't let go."

"Also he was very hungry," explained Uncle Douglas.

"So we fed him tea and haggis," said Aunt Doris.

Suddenly an extraordinary idea occurred to Daisy. "Didn't he have a mother?" she asked slowly.

Uncle Douglas unfolded a roll of green plastic and began to pump it up with a foot pump. "We tried to find her, but Loch Ness is very deep," he replied in a hollow voice.

For a moment nobody spoke.

"You mean Loopy is a baby Loch Ness monster!" croaked Jack.

Aunt Doris nodded. "So now you understand why we have to be so

careful," she said. "That's why
Hector McHandy insisted on
reading the tea leaves before we
arranged the rescue mission."

"The McHandys are very
superstitious," explained Uncle
Douglas, still pumping. "They
always consult their breakfast tea
leaves."

"So what did the tea leaves say?" asked Jack.

"They said our children had to help us," replied Aunt Doris. She beamed. "But since we don't have any, you were the next best thing."

"Besides, Loopy's quite long now and it will take four of us to carry him," added Uncle Douglas.

7. Something Rather Slippery

Uncle Douglas stopped pumping
and stood up.

Something that looked like a
huge baby Loch Ness monster with
yellow eyes lay on the ground.

Daisy's hands flew to her face.
"What's *that*?" she cried.

"It's a decoy monster to confuse
the SAD mob," said Aunt Doris.
"Now we must call Loopy!"

Jack and Daisy watched in
amazement as she knelt down at the
edge of a long narrow lake and
began to hum.

A moment later, three little
humps, a long green snout and two

yellow eyes rose out of the water.

Daisy grabbed a rock to stop herself fainting.

"Loopy!" squealed Aunt Doris. Quickly she held a piece of McHandy haggis in front of the baby monster's nose.

Loopy sniffed it and slithered out on to the rocks.

At the same time, Uncle Douglas slid the decoy monster into the lake.

"Which end shall we take?" whispered Jack.

"You take the middle, I'll carry his tail and Aunt Doris will feed him his bottle," whispered Uncle Douglas. "And if we meet the SAD mob, leave them to me."

So Jack and Daisy stumbled out of the cave and along the path with a baby Loch Ness Monster on their shoulders. He wasn't too heavy, but he was rather slippery and smelled of fish a lot.

They had almost reached the edge of the loch when a crowd of torches appeared round the corner.

It was the SAD mob!

"Switch off your lights," ordered Uncle Douglas. "We're a SAD advance party. We've got one monster. There's another in the cave."

"Two, eh?" squeaked a voice in the dark. "Hear that, boys? One on either side of the clubhouse chimney!"

"Exactly!" said Uncle Douglas.

"See you at the bottom."

"Righto!" said the squeaky voice.
"We won't be long!"

"Hurry!" muttered Uncle
Douglas to Jack and Daisy.

Five minutes later, there were
howls of rage and rocks bounced all
around them.

"Oh, no!" cried Aunt Doris.

"Don't you worry," said a gruff

voice. "I'm not called McHandy for
nothing!"

8. The Swing's All Yours!

Hector McHandy jumped out from behind a bush. He was carrying a huge bucket with **SUPERGLUE – EXTRA STRONG** written on the side.

"What are you going to do?" cried Daisy.

A tombstone grin sparkled in the moonlight. "Don't you worry, lassie," laughed Hector McHandy. "Let's just say, the SAD mob are heading for a sticky end."

And with that, he began to slop glue all over the narrow rocky path behind them.

"Look!" cried Aunt Doris. "Look! Down on the loch!"

Jack and Daisy looked.

Three huge humps were heading towards the shore!

They ran as fast as they could, but it wasn't fast enough for Loopy. It was almost as if he knew who was waiting for him. As they reached the shore, he squirmed out of their arms and leaped into the water.

Everyone watched as the three little humps zoomed over the loch to the three big humps. The water swirled and frothed. Both sets of humps sank side by side into the loch.

"Goodbye, Loopy!" cried Aunt Doris and Uncle Douglas. And they each sniffed a big sniff.

"Good luck!" shouted Jack and
Daisy.

Suddenly the night was filled with
cheering and roaring.

The roaring came from the SAD
mob who were stuck fast on the
narrow path.

The cheering came from the
McHandy clan.

The next thing they knew, Jack and Daisy, Uncle Douglas and Aunt Doris were being carried shoulder high!

Back at the castle, the huge panelled room was all laid out for a party. As Jack and Daisy walked in, Hector McHandy cocked an eye at the chandelier.

"The swing's all yours," he said
with a grin. "You did a great job!"

9. Nothing To Worry About

Mrs Primly-Proper was lying by a swimming pool doing absolutely nothing when the postcard arrived.

Beside her, Mr Primly-Proper was practising his golf swing with a toy golf club.

Mr Primly-Proper put down his club and read out the postcard. "Rescued a baby monster. Swung on a chandelier. Having an *incredible* time, love Jack and Daisy."

Mrs Primly-Proper jumped up with a start.

"Goodness gracious!" she cried. "What on earth is going on?"

"Nothing to worry about, dear," replied Mr Primly-Proper in a knowing voice. "Aunt Doris and Uncle Douglas must have taken the children to an adventure park."

He patted Mrs Primly-Proper's hand. "You know how Jack and Daisy like to make up exciting adventures."

Mrs Primly-Proper lay back on
her deckchair. "Of course they do,"
she sighed happily. "Now, shall we
have a cup of tea and see what's on
television?"

Mr Primly-Proper's eyes lit up.
"That's a good idea," he said.
"We'll have an exciting adventure
all of our own!"